Frango & Chicken

Written & Illustrated By Elena Stowell

Frango & Chicken © 2018 Elena Stowell. All rights reserved.

All illustrations are copyright of the author and illustrator and are also reproduced here in the spirit of publicity. Except for inclusion in a review, no part of this book may be reproduced in any form or by any means—electronic, mechanical, digital, photocopying, or recording—without permission in writing from author or publisher.

Published by *thewordverve inc.*
First Edition 2018

ISBN: 978-0-9992479-5-2 (hardback)

Library of Congress No.: 2017956587

Frango & Chicken
A Book with Verve by *thewordverve*

www.thewordverve.com

———————————

*Illustrations including cover by
by Elena Stowell*

*Book Interior Layout
by Ellen C. Gray*

To my parents,
who encourage
creativity in all forms.

- Elena

"Bom dia, Chicken. Good morning."

Frango and Chicken both like cereal for breakfast.

"Chicken, please go get my pencil and paper. I need to write a letter. *Não se preocupe.* Don't worry about it, Chicken. It's not impossible for you to do that."

"Remember the envelope...and the stamp!"

Frango and Chicken have many things to do today.

"*Vamos.* Let's go."

Frango and Chicken ride into town.
"You can hang on, Chicken!
Tudo é possível.
Everything is possible."

They ride over the river and past the market to the mailbox.

Opa! Frango stops too fast!

"Good job, Chicken! Thank you. *Obrigado*. Okay, now get up. It's time for work."

Frango and Chicken go to work in the *mercadinho*. Frango bags groceries. Chicken helps.

"What a mess! It's going to be impossible to clean this up."

"*Calma*, Chefe.
Ajuda-me, Chicken. Help me.
We can do this. *Tudo é possível.*"

"Oh, Chicken, look at you!"

*"Não se preocupe.
It's not impossible to
play futebol."*

They travel out of town, past the lake and close to the big city.

Jiu-jitsu is Frango's favorite sport.

Frango puts on his gi, a special uniform for jiu-jitsu. Chicken helps Frango tie his belt.

"Obrigado. Tudo é possível."

"It's nice that we can help each other. *Boa noite*, Chicken. Goodnight."

"Difficult does not mean impossible.
Difícil não significa impossível."

GLOSSARY

Ajuda-me: (AAz•hood•aa meh) - Help me.

Boa noite: (Boah noy•tee) - Good night.

Bom dia: (bohn dee•ah) - Good morning.

Calma: (kawma) - Take it easy!

Chefe: (shehf•ee) - Boss.

Difícil não significa impossível: (Deef•ees•eel nahn•oo seeg•neef •eek•a eeng•po•see•vel) - Difficult does not mean impossible.

Frango: (Frahn•goo) - Chicken.

Futebol: (foo•teh•bohl) - Soccer

Mercadinho: (merka•dee•nyo) - Grocery store.

Não se preocupe: (Nahn•oo se pre•o•koo•pay) Don't worry

Obrigado: (oh•bree•gahd•oo) - Thank you.

Opa!: (opa) - Oops!

Tudo é possível: (Tudu eh poo•see•veho•o) - Everything is possible.

Vamos: (Vah•moos) - We are going; Let's go.

TRANSLATION

INSPIRATION

Frango & Chicken Was Inspired by the True Story of Luciano "Frango" Mariano

Frango & Chicken was inspired by the true story of Luciano "Frango" Mariano. "I don't feel 'not normal,' I feel like ME." Luciano was three months old when he was burned in a fire that resulted in the amputation of both arms. "Sure, I was teased, but only by my friends, so it was all in good fun. They gave me the nickname Frango." Luciano was raised like the other kids in the neighborhood. He admits to being shy, but had all the same curiosities as his friends. "They helped me try the things they did . . . ride a bike, soccer . . . they introduced me to jiu-jitsu."

It was through the martial art of jiu-jitsu that the author, Elena Stowell, met Luciano in Rio de Janeiro, Brazil. "I want to be a world champion," he told her. Luciano

AS A YOUNG BOY

LUCIANO WITH HIS FRIENDS

WITH ELENA STOWELL IN RIO DE JANERIO, BRAZIL.

competes in the rooster weight division, 127.5 pounds or less (58kg). He trains locally several days a week with his professor, Paulo Marcio, and travels almost two hours by bus to train with Master Casquinha Guimaraes. "I feel fortunate to have jiu-jitsu in my life. On the mat, we are all the same. Yes, I use my feet to help me. The sweep that is in the book—it surprises my opponents. I grab their gi with one foot, pass it to my other foot, and pull them over."

He says, "It makes me feel good to know that people see me as an inspiration. I try to live my life by seeing all things as possible. Around me, I see people with two arms and two legs, good lives and health, but they complain. They put limits on themselves." Luciano teaches this life lesson by volunteering to help children participate in jiu-jitsu and stay off the streets.

Life in many parts of Brazil are described as difficult. When asked if he could change one thing, Luciano replies, "Participating in sports and martial arts is good for young people. It provides them many opportunities and can keep them from making bad choices. But here, there is no center for sports. We train with old mats on the ground. We need a space with low rent so children don't have to pay. Then they can learn the things they need to know for a good life—the things that sports can teach."

In 2014, with the help of the Carly Stowell Foundation, Hyperfly, Professor Jean Carlos, and the Challenged Athlete Foundation, Luciano traveled to the United States to train and compete. He hopes to travel more and share his story. "I don't have a pet chicken," he laughs, "but I have friends who act like Chicken."

LET'S TALK ABOUT THE BOOK!

1. Were you surprised when you realized that Frango has no hands, no arms below his elbows? Think about that. How you would do things differently? How would you pick something up? Brush your teeth? Eat?

2. Does Frango feel sorry for himself?

3. Does Chicken remind you of a best friend who will help you when you need it?

4. Have you ever watched or tried a martial art like jiu-jitsu?

5. What is the name of the uniform worn in jiu-jitsu? What uniforms or costumes have you worn or do you most want to wear?

6. Were you surprised that Frango can ride a bike? And that Chicken was able to mail the letter?

7. Where does Frango (Luciano) live?

8. Frango can speak two languages. Do you know any words in another language?

9. If you could write a book about someone who inspires you, who would you write about?

LET'S TALK ABOUT THE BOOK!

10. Have you ever thought something was going to be impossible to do, but tried anyway? What happened? What did you learn about yourself?

11. Who thinks it's impossible to do things: Chicken or Frango? How do you encourage a friend?

12. The illustrations in the book are made with pieces of paper and glue. How do you like to illustrate pictures? If you could add a picture to the story what would it look like?

13. Frango is a nickname. Do you have a nickname? How did you get it?

14. What do you like to eat for breakfast?

15. Have you ever written a letter to someone? Have you ever addressed a letter?

ABOUT THE AUTHOR

PHOTO: PHOTOGRAPHY OF OZ

Elena Stowell is an author, science teacher, and Brazilian jiu-jitsu practitioner. When she is writing and illustrating, Elena can be found at a table with a real #2 pencil and her favorite pair of scissors buried in paper scraps, dried paint, glue-sticks, broken toothpicks, and half-empty coffee cups. "Working in collage puts me in my happy place, which is pretty messy."

Elena is the award-winning author of *Flowing with the Go: A Jiu-Jitsu Journey of the Soul*. She is co-founder of the non-profit Carly Stowell Foundation and director of the JamminBJJ Give the Gift of a Gi program. Her volunteer work helps make sports and music participation affordable and accessible to children and adults around the world. She is a member of the Society of Children's Book Writers and Illustrators.

Elena is available for author talks, book signings, and other events, particularly those that highlight diversity, overcoming obstacles, and positivity. You can reach her through her website www.elenastowell.com or through her publisher www.thewordverve.com.

CPSIA information can be obtained
at www.ICGtesting.com
Printed in the USA
BVHW02*1142180518
516663BV00001B/1/P